THE PORTAL

BY: G. PENN

OTHER WORKS BY G. PENN:

*The Island, Book Two of the
Museum Mysteries*

*The Cave, Book Three of
the Museum Mysteries*

PROLOGUE

B AST SAT ON THE WINDOWSILL, peering in at the three girls. It was cold, but her thick fur kept her warm.

"Maximus is right," she purred to herself. "They will do just fine."

The tallest of the three girls turned and stared out the window.

Bast jumped to the ground and quickly hid in the woods. "Soon, my young friends. Soon we will meet." She purred.

CHAPTER 1

COUSINS

I N BED AT NOMMY AND Pa's, Claira yawned and snuggled closer to her sister, Ariel. She reached over Ariel and touched their cousin Kimberly on the arm. None of them were asleep yet, and she wondered if Ariel and Kimberly were as sleepy as she was. She yawned again and turned towards the window. Was it snowing? Nommy had said it might snow tonight.

Staring at the window, Claira saw two huge yellow eyes staring back at her. She sat up, pushed the blankets off, and ran to the window. Ariel and Kimberly sat up in bed. Claira turned around to look at them, put her fingers to her mouth, and whispered, "Shh." There was a cat sitting on the windowsill. Was Nommy's cat Jasper trying to get in? He roamed the fields during the day, but Nommy always brought him inside at night. It was dark outside, and Jasper was dark grey with stripes.

Just as she got to the window, the cat disappeared from the windowsill. Claira pressed her face against the window but couldn't see anything except the branches of a big tree. It was cloudy, and Nommy and Pa lived in a big house in the country where there were no streetlights. The only light was from the two ladybug night-lights on each side of the bed.

"I hope Nommy doesn't forget Jasper tonight. It hasn't started snowing, but it's really cloudy and cold," Claira said. She turned away from the window, ran back to bed, and slipped under the covers beside Ariel. Nommy had put lots of warm blankets on the bed.

Kimberly, on the other side of Ariel, grabbed the blanket and pulled it towards her.

"Kimberly, stop it!" said Claira.

"You pulled it off of me!" said Kimberly.

Ariel sat up, pushed the blanket down, and climbed over Claira to get out of bed.

"What...?" Claira asked.

Ariel walked over to the dresser, picked up the ornaments Nommy had bought them at the Walters Art Gallery that day, and re-arranged them. Their grandmother Nommy took them to the museum every year to see the Christmas tree and exhibits. Claira's mom and Aunt Elisabeth, Kimberly's mom, had gone to the museum with them.

Ariel had placed the St. Nicholas ornament first, the Bast ornament second, and the black Labrador ornament last.

"Why'd you do that?" Claira asked her.

Ariel turned around and pointed at Claira. "You chose St. Nicholas, and you're six and the oldest, so yours is first. Kimberly chose Bast, and she is six, too. I'm only four, so my ornament is the last."

Ariel turned back around and picked up the Labrador ornament and peered at the eyes. She gave it a quick kiss. "His name is Max, like Nommy and Pa's dog," Ariel said. Tears filled her eyes as she looked at Claira. "I miss Max, Claira. I wish my ornament had a red eye like Max did," said Ariel.

Claira jumped out of bed, and ran over to Ariel. She gave her a big hug. Nommy and Pa's dog Max had died recently, and it was Ariel's first experience with saying good-bye to a special pet.

"Max was blind in one eye, but he didn't have a red eye, Ariel," Claira said.

"It was red. It was," Ariel insisted. "Daddy told me Mommy said Max had a red terminator eye. What's a terminator eye?"

Kimberly had climbed out of bed and was standing by Claira.

Claira hugged Ariel. "Daddy was joking. Uncle William teased Mommy that Max's fake eye was red and he could see in the dark like the Terminator. *The Terminator* is a movie about someone with red eyes who can see everything. Daddy said it's a scary movie, and we have to be older to watch it."

Claira picked up Kimberly's Bast ornament. It looked like a cat and was the symbol of an Egyptian goddess. Claira had learned about Bast when she studied her in school. Kimberly went to a different school, but she had told Claira they studied Egypt, too. Claira and Ariel had two cats, but Kimberly had six! She told Claira she got the Bast ornament because she loved her cats.

Nommy had given them ten dollars each to spend in the gift shop. She told them to use five dollars to buy a gift for someone and five dollars to buy something for themselves. They had each chosen an ornament they liked on the tall Christmas tree at the Walters and bought a copy of it in the gift shop. They had also chosen matching bracelets, just like last Christmas, when they had visited the museum.

The bracelets were made of thin strands of woven leather with a black cat in the center. The lady behind the counter in the gift shop said they had just gotten the bracelets in the store that week.

"Let's get a new bracelet each year," Claira had suggested. "See? I still have mine from last year. Let's see if we can get enough bracelets to cover our arms!"

"Ah, I lost mine," Kimberly said.

"Me too!" Ariel said.

"That's okay. I'll put mine from last year on this arm, and we'll put all the new ones we get on the other arm." Claira had moved last year's bracelet to her left arm, and she'd left both bracelets on when they went to bed.

Claira stared at Kimberly's Bast ornament and noticed something. She picked it up and held it beside the new bracelet on her right arm.

"Kimberly, your ornament looks just

like the cat on our new bracelets!" Claira said.

Kimberly and Ariel looked at their bracelets and the Bast ornament.

"Yeah, that's cool!" Kimberly said, yawning.

"I still like Max best," said Ariel as she turned around and ran back to bed.

Claira put the Bast ornament back on the dresser. She grabbed Kimberly's hand and pulled her towards the bed. "I'm sleepy, and we need to straighten the blanket," Claira said.

Ariel had already climbed back into the middle of the bed and snuggled under the covers. Kimberly and Claira tugged on the blankets, getting them as even as possible. Claira and Kimberly climbed into bed on either side of Ariel, and Claira leaned over and gave Ariel a kiss. She reached over and touched Kimberly on the arm. She snuggled under the blankets and pulled them up to her chin.

Ariel sat up and lifted her pillow. She pulled three clementines out from under her pillow and handed one to Claira. "I'm hungry. I have one for Kimberly, too. Nommy won't be angry, will she?"

"Yummy! Thanks, Ariel. No, Nommy won't be angry. Give me the peelings, and I'll put them on the table by me.

We'll throw them away tomorrow, before Nommy comes in the room." Claira turned to Kimberly to tell her Ariel had clementines, but Kimberly was already asleep.

It had been a long day.

Claira yawned and handed the clementine back to Ariel. "I'm sleepy. We'll eat them for breakfast." Claira smiled as Ariel put it back under her pillow.

CHAPTER 2

THE LIGHT

I N THE MIDDLE OF THE night, Claira sat up in bed. She was cold. Kimberly had pulled all the blankets to one side again.

Had it started snowing yet? Claira jumped out of bed and went to the window, but it was too dark outside to see. She rubbed the windowpane and looked again, but she couldn't see anything.

She went back to the bed, climbed in beside Ariel, and reached over and grabbed the edge of the blanket, tugging on it until she had enough to cover herself. Ariel felt warm beside her, and she snuggled closer. She fell back to sleep but soon woke up again.

Claira looked towards the window to see if the cat had come back. She sat up and looked around the room.

Sometimes Claira, Ariel, and Kimberly would climb up on a chair and open the door of the wall closet. They would move the blankets so they could sit in the closet. It was big enough for them to all sit down and read and color. But they *never* closed the door. They always propped the door open with a chair and took flashlights with them, just in case the door accidentally closed. Nommy told Claira Aunt Elisabeth used to do the same thing when she was a little girl.

Claira heard the big clock in the hall. No cats. She lay down and snuggled under the blanket. She counted the number of times it rang. *Twelve. Midnight.* Nommy and Pa were asleep. Yawning, she closed her eyes and tried to go back to sleep. Nommy wouldn't like it if she woke Kimberly and Ariel up. Besides, she was tired.

Claira sat up in bed again. Something had awakened her. There! A circle of light on the door of the closet.

"Nommy?" she whispered. Sometimes Nommy would come in with a flashlight to check on them when they were asleep.

"Nommy!" Claira whispered again. Nommy didn't answer. The light got bigger.

Kimberly sat up in bed, rubbing her

eyes and looking at Claira. "Quiet. I'm sleepy."

Ariel turned over and pulled the pillow over her head.

Claira pointed to the closet door. "A light. There!" she whispered to Kimberly.

"Maybe it's Nommy checking on us," she said.

"Ariel, wake up!" Claira shook Ariel's shoulder and pulled the blanket off Kimberly.

"*Claira*! Stop it," Kimberly grumbled. She grabbed the blanket and pulled it over her head. "Don't touch my blanket."

Ariel sat up and rubbed her eyes. "I'm cold."

Claira didn't answer them as she stared at the light, a circle with something at the top of the circle. It was growing bigger.

She reached over and pulled the blanket down off Kimberly, again. "Wake up."

Claira called out, "Nommy, is that you? Pa? Nommy?"

"I'm scared, Claira," Ariel said.

Kimberly whispered, "That's because you're a baby, Ariel!"

"Shish, Kimberly! She's not a baby. And I'm scared, too," said Claira.

All three girls stared at the light as it

kept growing. The light was in a circle, but in the center of the light was a dark circle. *Really* dark.

CHAPTER 3

BAST

"KIMBERLY, GET UP AND OPEN the door! We need Nommy!" Claira whispered.

"Me? Why me? *You* open the door! You're older," Kimberly whispered back, pulling the covers over her head.

Tears ran down Ariel's face. "I want Pa... Pa." She gulped, pushed the covers back, and was climbing over Claira to get to the door when something jumped out from the darkness in the shining circle. The circle closed, and the only light in the room was again from the two ladybug night-lights.

Ariel shrank back beside Claira.

It was a large black cat.

"Do not be afraid," the cat said. "I am your friend."

The voice was beautiful.

Ariel, Claira, and Kimberly stared. A cat that talked, and Claira understood what was said?

"Ariel, Kimberly! Did you hear that? The cat talked, and I understood!" Claira whispered.

"Uh huh," whispered Kimberly. Ariel nodded.

"I am Bast. You know who I am, or I would not have been summoned," the cat said.

"Summoned?" Claira asked.

"Sent for, called for," the cat replied. "Hold out your arms and look at your bracelets. Do you see the cat symbol on your bracelet? That's me. Bast." The cat's long black tail flicked back and forth. "You'll notice I'm a lot better looking in real life."

Ariel, Claira, and Kimberly looked at their bracelets. They looked at the cat again. She did look like the cat on their bracelets. All three girls slowly nodded yes.

"Cat got your tongue?" The cat laughed softly. "That's a joke, you know. Or are you too young to know that's a joke?"

Ariel turned to Claira. "Cats can't talk!" Ariel whispered to Claira.

The cat waved its tail and arched its back. "This cat does, little Ariel."

Claira stared at the cat. "Ariel is my little sister. Don't make fun of her. She's right. Cats *don't* talk. How do you know her name?"

"I know all your names. You're Claira." The cat daintily lifted its right paw and pointed at Kimberly. "You're Kimberly, and I know Claira is four months older than you. Ariel is the youngest. You may call me Bast."

"Huh? How do you know our names...? Bast, like the Egyptian goddess?" Claira stammered.

"Yes, *that* Bast. Magic, of course! How do you think I'm able to talk to you? Hurry! Time is short. We must leave soon if we are to find him," replied the cat.

"Ah, Miss Bast. Leave? Find him? Find who?" Claira asked.

"Bast will do just fine. No 'Miss.' St. Nicholas of course, and his head elf Herbie. They have disappeared, and we need your help," Bast said.

"St. Nicholas? Lost? You want *us* to help you?" Kimberly asked.

The cat settled down on her haunches, head held high and slender neck stretched out. She took her left paw and pulled on the collar around her neck.

"Kimberly, you chose a figure of a cat for your decoration. Claira chose St. Nicholas. And Ariel chose the black Labrador decoration. And you all chose matching bracelets with my symbol, the cat, on the bracelets," Bast said. "Look at my collar. What does it look like?"

All three girls looked at the collar around Bast's neck.

Kimberly reached out and touched it. "It looks like our bracelets!"

"It not only looks like your bracelets, it is identical to them," Bast said.

"You mean that's how you found us?" Claira asked.

"Not found. Connected. Whatever you want to call it," Bast said.

"Yes... but..." Claira stammered.

Ariel pulled the covers up to her neck. "I'm scared, Claira. I want Mommy."

Bast reached out and touched Ariel's knee with her paw. "I will protect you, little Ariel. And besides, you chose the black Labrador. He is very powerful and very wise. He will help us. I don't know why you three girls were chosen to help find St. Nicholas, but I know how. The bracelets had a spell on them to call me if they were chosen by three children who were related. You are cousins. Oh, and one had to be a redhead!"

"Where are we going? When will we get back?" Kimberly asked as she pulled on a strand of her red hair.

"It is after midnight. Today is December twenty-fourth. You will be back here *today*, before the sun rises."

"How... come back the same day we leave?" Claira asked.

"Time travel. You know what that is, don't you? St. Nicholas needs our help, as do the children. We have to go," Bast said.

"What happens if we don't go?" Kimberly asked as she grabbed Ariel's pillow and hugged it tightly. Claira stared at the three clementines that had been under Ariel's pillow. She turned back to look at Bast.

"I don't know," said Bast, "but I know St. Nicholas needs our help. He is locked away. If we don't free him, there won't be any Christmas!"

"Why do we have to go? If you're special and can talk and time travel, you can help him," Claira said.

Bast purred and daintily licked her paw. "Yes, I am special. But we need your help. Didn't you listen to me? You were chosen because you're related and because you chose *my* bracelet. Only you three can help Santa."

Claira stared at Bast's long black tail, which slowly flicked back and forth.

Ariel reached over and grabbed Claira's hand. Kimberly grabbed Ariel's other hand.

"When will we be back? What if Nommy comes looking for us?" Kimberly whispered.

"Your Nommy won't even know you're gone. You keep forgetting the time travel. We'll be there and back before anyone misses you!"

Claira turned her head and looked at Ariel and Kimberly. "We have to go. What if the cat is right, and Santa can't come?"

Ariel held tightly to Claira's hand. She snuggled closer to Claira. "Don't let go of my hand."

Kimberly looked at Claira and nodded slowly. She grabbed the clementines that had been under Ariel's pillow and stuffed them in her pocket.

"Good, girls. Ready?" Bast asked as she jumped onto Ariel's lap. "Don't let go of each other's hands, or you might get lost!"

Bast started purring. The temperature of the room dropped. The shining circle appeared again on the door of the wall closet. In the center of the circle it was dark, but Claira could see a light shining in the distance. The girls held tightly to one another's hands.

"Claira, don't let go!" Ariel yelled.

Suddenly they were flying through the air. Bast had jumped off Ariel's lap and was in front of them. Claira saw Bast had sprouted wings. Ariel, Claira, and Kimberly entered the shining circle behind Bast. The circle silently closed as they stepped in.

CHAPTER 4

SNOW

"KIMBERLY! ARIEL!" YELLED CLAIRA. "Claira. Turn around. We're behind you. What...?" Kimberly stared. Claira wasn't in pajamas. She was bundled up in a thick red winter coat with a fur-lined hood. She had boots on, like the ones Kimberly wore when she went out to play in the snow, with black snow pants that tucked into them. Her hands were in thick gloves.

Kimberly held her own hands out and stared at the gloves on them. She looked down at her feet. She then looked at Ariel. They were dressed alike, except for the color of their coats. Claira's was red, Kimberly's was blue, and Ariel's was green. The clothing was a good thing, because it was snowing big, thick, wet snowflakes.

Kimberly's gloves had a picture of St. Nicholas on the right hand. On the left glove was a picture of a black cat and a black dog. The pictures looked exactly like the ornaments they had gotten in the gift shop at the Walters!

Claira hugged Ariel and Kimberly. She pulled their hoods off their heads. "I was holding Ariel's hand and then I wasn't. I was scared I had lost you."

Kimberly heard a purring sound and turned around. It sounded like Bast. "Did you hear that?" she asked Claira and Ariel.

"Sounds like Bast," said Claira.

The purring stopped. Kimberly heard laughter and a soft voice, but she saw no one.

"You are not alone," Bast said. "I have changed and wanted to warn you before you saw me. I am at my most beautiful now, but you might have been startled or frightened if I did not warn you."

"Where are you? You told us you were going to protect us!" Kimberly yelled.

"I am here, but I needed to prepare you. Close your eyes, and do not open them until I tell you to," Bast said.

"I'm not closing my eyes!" Kimberly said.

"You have to. I can't do this invisible

bit for long. I'm still practicing. Have you ever tried it? I'm telling you, it's hard to do!"

Invisible? Kimberly looked at Claira and Ariel. "It's her voice. It's Bast. Close your eyes. We need her help to get home."

All three girls squeezed their eyes shut.

"Now! Open your eyes," Bast said.

Kimberly opened her eyes, screamed, and jumped back, knocking Ariel down. Claira reached down and grabbed Ariel's hand, pulling her to her feet. Ariel held tightly to Claira's hand.

Standing in front of them was the biggest cat Kimberly had ever seen.

The cat shook herself from head to toe. Her tail was standing straight up with the tip slightly bent. She was the size of a panther.

The cat faced the girls. The cat's eyes were yellow, just like Bast's eyes, but they were huge.

"Bast?" Kimberly whispered.

"Of course," Bast said. "I can do lots more."

"More?" Kimberly asked. "You can get bigger?"

"Not bigger. Different shapes. Close your eyes. I'll show you," Bast said.

"Why do we have to close our eyes?" Kimberly asked.

"You can't watch. That's not allowed. I have to concentrate, and I can't concentrate if I am being watched. Turn around if you want, but no peeking!"

All three girls turned their backs to Bast. The snow was falling in heavy, wet flakes. Kimberly peered into the distance, but the snow was so thick it was like trying to look through a soft, white blanket. All she could see was snow.

"Now can we turn around, Bast?" asked Kimberly. She knew it had only been a few minutes, but it seemed like forever.

"Ta dah," Bast said. "What do you think? Do you like this better?"

Claira, Kimberly, and Ariel turned back around and stared. Standing in front of them was a really pretty woman, wearing a long black coat, jeans, and knee-high black boots. She was tall, and her long, shiny black hair, which was plaited into a single braid, fell over her right shoulder down to the middle of her chest.

Claira grabbed Ariel's hand and pulled Ariel with her as she stepped closer to the woman. She stared at the braid. "That looks like a cat's tail. And your eyes are still yellow!" said Claira.

Claira let go of Ariel's hand and reached up and touched Bast's braid.

Bast smiled. "My eyes always stay the same. My shape I can change, but not everything. It would be too creepy if my tail were poking out my pants. Sort of hard to wear skinny jeans!"

"Yeah, you're right. That would be weird. And it would be scary to see a panther walking down the street," Kimberly said.

CHAPTER 5

MAXIMUS

Bast looked at Claira. Claira was pointing to the figures of the dog and cat with her right hand. "Um, Bast? You're the cat ornament, right?" said Claira.

Bast smiled at her. "I'm not the ornament. The ornament is my symbol. You do know what a symbol means, don't you?"

"Yeah. But there's a dog with you. Where's the dog?" Claira asked.

"I was going to tell you about him. He can be a little bit scary. You needed to know you could trust me first before I introduced him," Bast said.

Ariel stared at Bast. She grabbed Claira's hand and whispered, "More scary...?"

Bast knelt down in the snow in front

of Ariel. "You have been very brave, little Ariel. He is very large. Almost as large as a horse."

Bast stood up. She looked off into the distance and waved her hand.

She turned to face the girls. "You will meet him in a few minutes."

"Is he invisible?" Kimberly asked.

Bast smiled. "No, he can't disappear. He is special in other ways. He can run over the snow and make no tracks or sounds. He is big enough for all three of you to sit on his back. And, of course, there is his eye."

"What about his eye?" Kimberly asked. She moved closer to Ariel and Claira.

"It's spe—"

A booming voice sounded behind Bast, interrupting her. "I am Maximus. Do not be afraid."

"Girls, meet Maximus," said Bast as she turned around to the sound of the loud voice. Reaching up with her right hand she gently touched the muzzle of Maximus, who looked like a huge black Labrador retriever. Turning back to the girls, she smiled. She and Maximus were best friends and had been on many adventures together.

"Yikes!" Tears began to fall from Ariel's eyes.

"You scared my little sister," Claira

yelled. She stomped her foot and pried Ariel's hand loose. She moved closer to the dog and stared at him. She stood on her tiptoes and looked at his eyes.

Maximus's right eye was dark brown but the left eye was bright red. He was black all over, except for a little bit of white fur under his neck.

"You are very brave, young lady," Maximus said. "Most people are afraid of my size."

"You made my little sister cry," Claira whispered. "I have to take care of her."

"You are a good big sister, Claira. Ariel is a lucky little girl," Maximus said.

Bast went to him and put her hand on the huge dog's left shoulder. She turned around and spoke to the girls. "We need the help of Maximus. We have far to travel, and he will give us a ride. He is very gentle but will protect us if we are in danger."

Claira stood on tiptoes and touched Maximus's cheek.

"Are you a Labrador retriever? Nommy and Pa had a black Labrador retriever, but he wasn't a giant," Claira said.

"Yes, I am a giant, aren't I? I am a friend of Bast. I was sent to help and protect you."

"We're lucky it's not my cousin

Anabas," Bast said. "He's not a nice dog.
"

"Huh?" Kimberly asked. "Anabas? He's scary?"

"Bast, let's not bring him up," Maximus said. "The girls have enough to contend with now. Don't you think a talking cat who changes shape and a giant dog who leaves no footprints are enough for one story? "

"Sorry, Maximus," Bast said. "You're right."

"I want to go home," Ariel whispered. "I want to go back to Nommy's house."

"But we need Bast's help to get home," Claira said. "And Bast said we're supposed to help St. Nicholas."

"Where is St. Nicholas?" Claira asked.

"Do you know the legend of St. Nicholas?" Maximus asked.

"We call him Santa Claus," Kimberly said. "But my teacher said children in other countries call him other names, like St. Nicholas. She said he lived a long time ago and had lots of money. He gave presents, food, and money to people who needed it."

"Your teacher is right," Maximus said. "There are many stories about St. Nicholas. One story tells of him giving three gold balls to three poor girls so they would have money to get married."

"What about their mom and dad? Couldn't they give the girls money to get married?" Claira asked.

"They were very poor," Bast said. It costs a lot to get married. I'm glad I'm a cat and don't have to worry about a wedding!"

Maximus smiled at Bast. Bast smiled back at him.

But then Maximus stopped smiling. "The gold balls were very valuable. Trolls love gold, too. Three trolls have taken St. Nicholas and locked him away until he agrees to give them some gold balls, as well."

"Does Santa have gold balls to give them?" Claira asked.

"That's the problem," Bast said. "He's big into presents now. But the trolls think he has the gold balls and have locked him away."

"But how can we help him?" Kimberly asked. "We're just little girls. We don't have any gold balls!"

"Maximus and I were sent to bring you to help Santa," Bast said.

"Sent?" Kimberly asked. "Who sent you?"

"A message," Maximus answered. "A pigeon delivered a rhyme to both of us."

"A pigeon?" Claira said. "What about a phone or the Internet?"

Maximus smiled at the girls. "They don't have the Internet at the North Pole. I'm not sure they have phones."

"The North Pole," Kimberly whispered. "Are we at the North Pole, where Santa and the elves live?"

Ariel spoke up. "Claira, what's a rhyme? I want to go home."

"Yeah, what about the message from the pigeon?" Claira asked. "I want to see it. What did it say?"

"You can't see the message," Bast said. "The pigeons tell you their messages in person."

"Yeah, right," Claira said. "Like pigeons can talk."

"Why not?" Bast asked. "You're talking to me, and I'm a cat. Pigeons are smart."

"Ah," Claira said. "But I want to know what the message said."

Bast held her right index finger to the side of her head as she focused on remembering the poem.

"Santa will be saved on Christmas Eve
By bracelet and by blood, three girls will intertwine—
A redhead and two blondes will be assigned
The children of the world will not grieve—

With the help of the talking cat and the red-eyed canine."

"I think that's right," Bast said.

"Close enough," said Maximus. He smiled at Bast. "She always has trouble remembering rhymes!"

"Huh?" Kimberly asked. "By bracelet and blood, three girls will intertwine?" Before anyone could answer, she yelled, "I get it. We're cousins and we have the same bracelet! I have red hair and they have blonde hair!"

"Shhh," Claira said. "Don't yell. It scares Ariel."

"Girls, we have to go," Bast said. "Santa has a long day ahead of him, and we have to get him back home so he can supervise packing the sleigh."

"Bast will help you onto my back," Maximus said as he stretched and wagged his tail.

Bast knelt beside Maximus. She moved her left foot so it was flat on the ground and patted her left knee. "Grab my neck and step up on my knee," she said. "I'll give you a boost onto his back."

Claira took Ariel's hand and walked over to Bast. "I'll be first, Ariel. You can be next and sit behind me. Kimberly will sit behind you. We'll protect you."

Bast helped all three girls settle onto

Maximus's back. She told them to grab his fur with both hands. "Your gloves are special. They will not let you let go of his fur as long as he is moving."

She stood up and brushed the snow off her pants. "Now I need for you to close your eyes."

"Yeesh, here we go again," Kimberly said. "What will you be this time, Bast?"

"Close your eyes, girls," Maximus said. "Christmas Eve will be here soon."

Bast stared at the girls, checking to make sure their eyes were closed. "Good girls," she said.

Bast closed her eyes and... within five seconds a black cat with beautiful yellow eyes jumped onto Maximus's back in front of Claira.

Settling down onto the big dog's back she gently held onto his neck, snuggling up against Claira. Bast closed her eyes as they raced across the snowy landscape. Maximus did not need directions.

CHAPTER 6

FLYING ACROSS THE SNOW

Claira, Ariel, and Kimberly held tightly to the thick, black fur as they flew across the snow. Claira felt Ariel snuggled tightly up against her back, and she trusted Kimberly to snuggle behind Ariel and shield her back. Claira squinted her eyes to keep out the snow, opening them occasionally to look around at the landscape. Other than Bast's soft purring, there was no sound—not even the sound of the huge dog running through the snow.

Bast was right: Maximus left no footprints in the snow. Claira turned around and peered behind them. Certainly she should have seen an impression of footprints. Maximus was very large and had to be very heavy. Claira no idea of time—only of the warmth of the huge dog's body and the darkness of the night. They had entered a forest and were weaving in and out between the huge tree trunks.

Claira felt Maximus start to climb. She opened her eyes and brushed the snow off her face. "We're climbing," she whispered.

Claira turned, reached around Ariel, and punched Kimberly on the arm. "Open your eyes," she whispered to Ariel and Kimberly. It was still dark, but Claira could tell the trees were not as big, and there were not as many as there had been when they had entered the forest.

"We're going up a mountain," Bast said. "Wait until you see what's on the other side."

Maximus did not slow down, even though the climb became steeper. Claira felt as if they were flying. She looked down at Maximus's side to make sure Maximus had not sprouted wings like Bast had when they went through the portal.

"No wings," Claira murmured. She quickly shut her eyes again. It was too scary to look at the ground flying beneath their feet. "When will we get there?" Claira yelled to Bast.

"Soon," replied Bast. "It is easy to lose

track of time when you're on Maximus, but it has only been twenty minutes. And don't yell! I'm a cat, you know. My hearing is excellent, if I say so myself—just like my eyesight!"

Claira couldn't tell how long they'd been traveling, but it felt like only a few minutes. She wondered if time was the same when they were with Bast.

"Open your eyes, girls," Bast said over her shoulder. "We're almost there."

Claira felt Maximus slowing down. She opened her eyes.

Maximus came to a complete stop.

Bast jumped down and walked around to stand behind him. "Eyes closed!"

"Not again!" Kimberly said.

"Yep, sorry," Bast said.

All three girls squeezed their eyes closed. Claira reached around and pulled Ariel closer to her. Kimberly pressed against Ariel's back.

"Now can we open our eyes?" Kimberly didn't wait for an answer from Bast. She opened her eyes and turned around.

Bast the cat was gone. Bast the woman was standing beside Maximus, dressed exactly as she had been before their ride on Maximus.

"Slide your right leg over, and I'll help you get down." Bast put her arms around Kimberly's waist and helped her to the ground. She did the same for Ariel and Claira.

"Follow me," Bast said. "I have a surprise. Maximus will wait here for us."

She led the girls through the snow, holding Ariel's hand. Claira and Kimberly walked behind her, holding hands. The snow was deep but with a thin, hardened crust. Claira looked at Ariel's small boot prints. It looked as if she was walking alone. Bast left no prints in the snow.

Claira reached out and touched Bast on the sleeve. Fur, as soft as the fur on a Persian cat. It was silky and glossy black. She felt as though she was petting her cat, Emily, but the fur was even softer. Claira whispered, "It feels like my aunt's mink coat. She got my uncle to buy it but is afraid to wear it. Someone yelled at her when she wore it to a party about three years ago. Called her an animal killer for killing all the little minks."

Bast turned her head, stopped, and smiled at Claira. "It *is* softer than mink." Her smiled turned to a frown. "Your aunt wasn't the animal killer, but if she really knew how they raised mink and slaughtered them for their coats, I am sure she would not wear the coat."

Claira's aunt with the mink coat was Kimberly's mother. Claira squeezed Kimberly's hand.

They walked for about fifteen minutes, to the crest of a hill. Claira noticed the trees had thinned out and were skinnier than they were when they were in the forest.

Bast stopped, lifted her arms, palms up, and spread her arms. "Ta-dah!"

Claira, Ariel, and Kimberly crowded around Bast. Claira saw they were overlooking a valley. Far below, she could see lights twinkling. It appeared as if there were thousands of lights twinkling in the night.

"There. That is where St. Nicholas lives and where he has a workshop," Bast said.

Claira stared. It looked as though it was very far away.

CHAPTER 7

THE VILLAGE

"THE NORTH POLE? ARE WE at the North Pole? That's where Santa lives," Claira said.

"North Pole, South Pole—who cares? That is Santa's village," Bast said.

"But...how...?" Claira stammered.

"Claira, we're talking to a cat who has wings, and we rode on a dog who doesn't leave footprints in the snow," Kimberly said. "And the cat changes to a person whenever she wants to! I don't know, but if Bast says we're at Santa's village, we must be."

Ariel tugged on Claira's sleeve. "I want to go home."

Bast knelt on her knees and put her hands on Ariel's shoulders. "We will go home, little Ariel. I promise you. You want to help Santa, though, don't you?"

Ariel hung her head. "We're little girls. Why do we have to help Santa? Why can't you and Maximus help Santa?"

Bast gently lifted Ariel's head and smiled at her. "Yes, you are little girls, but you are special little girls. You are blood related and have the special bracelet. Maximus and I are here to help and protect you, but we don't have the bond you three have. Santa needs *your* help."

Claira looked at Kimberly and said, "We need to talk, Bast."

Bast stood up and faced the three of them. "All right, shoot. We'll talk."

"No, not you," Claira said. "Kimberly, Ariel, and I need to talk. Ariel may be little, but she has the right to decide, too."

Bast smiled. "Put me in my place, right? Okay, I'll let you discuss it privately and decide. I'll be close in case you need me." She turned and walked towards the tree line.

Bast walked until she was about twenty feet from the three girls. She turned and waved at them. "Is this far enough?"

"Huh? Yeah, I guess so," Claira replied.

"What if she has special hearing?"

Kimberly asked. "Cats can hear really good. I know mine do. Hear things in the grass, like snakes."

"Yeah, you're right," Claira whispered. "But I don't want her disappearing and leaving us here by ourselves. That would be scary. I want to be able to see her. We need her to get back home." She grabbed Ariel's hand and drew her close.

Ariel's face was flushed, and there were tears in her eyes. Claira wasn't sure if it was from the ride on Maximus in the cold air or if she was getting ready to cry. "I'm scared, Claira. I want to go home. Don't let Bast leave. Who will take care of us?"

"I'll take care of you, and Kimberly will, too. We won't let anything happen to you," Claira said.

Kimberly moved closer to Ariel and Claira. She tugged the glove on her right hand, pulling it off. She reached under the sleeve of the thick coat and pulled her bracelet down her wrist. "What if I take the bracelet off? Will we be back home with Nommy and Pa?"

"No, don't do it!" Claira yelled. "What if we don't go back?"

"Don't!" whispered Ariel. Big tears began to drop from Ariel's eyes.

"See what you did, Kimberly! You

made Ariel cry," Claira said in a loud whisper.

Kimberly's face flushed red. She had red hair and was fair skinned, and whenever she got excited or upset, her face got red. Tears welled in her eyes. "You yelled, Claira! You made Ariel cry! And I want to go home, too," said Kimberly.

"I'm scared, too," Claira said. "But we need to stay together. We need to take care of Ariel. I dunno. I'm scared if Bast leaves or we take off the bracelets, we won't *ever* get home. And Maximus— we need him, too." Claira put her arm around Ariel and hugged her tightly.

Kimberly hung her head and closed her eyes. A tear rolled out from beneath a long lash, and she sniffed. She rubbed her nose with her gloved hand. She moved closer to Claira. "*You* decide. You're always telling me you're older than me!"

Claira stomped her foot in the snow. "Only four months! We have to all decide, not just me!"

Ariel stopped crying and huddled close to Claira. Kimberly tugged her glove back on her hand.

"Let's ask Bast what happens if we take the bracelets off. She'll know. Maybe we'll just be back home with Nommy and Pa if we do," Claira said.

Ariel nodded. Kimberly was quiet for a minute.

"But what if she says we can't take them off?" Kimberly asked. "What if they won't come off? We told her we were going to decide if we would help Santa. Will he come on Christmas?"

"I don't know, Kimberly. Bast knows about the bracelets. We have to ask her," said Claira. "I won't yell if you don't, Kimberly. It scares Ariel. Okay?"

Kimberly wiped the dampness from her cheeks and nodded yes.

Claira kneeled beside Ariel in the snow, like Bast had. She gave her a hug and kissed her cheek. "Ariel, I know you're scared and want to go home to Nommy and Pa. But we need to think about Santa. We might be the only ones who can help him. Tonight is Christmas Eve, and he might not be able to deliver special presents if we don't help him. We have to be grown up and decide what to do."

"I don't want to be grown up," Ariel said. "I'm little. Mommy and Daddy and Nommy and Pa are grown-ups."

"Kimberly and I will take care of you,

Ariel. We won't let anything happen to you," said Claira.

"Okay, I guess," Ariel whispered. "I want to help Santa. They're lots of little kids who don't have a big sister or cousin to help them. They need Santa to bring them special things."

Claira nodded slowly. "We have to help Santa. You know, like we always help our moms buy special gifts for other children who don't have moms or dads to buy them things like warm coats and hats."

Claira hugged Ariel tightly and stood up. She hugged Kimberly and tried to give her a kiss on the cheek, but Kimberly pushed her away.

"No kisses! You're only four months older than me!" Kimberly said.

"Sheesh, first you say I'm older, then you say I'm not! Make up your mind!" Claira said, but she was smiling at Kimberly.

"Okay, let's tell Bast we'll help. But first I'm going to ask her what happens if we take our bracelets off right now!" Claira said. "Bast! Bast!"

Bast walked across the snow towards the girls and stopped in front of them.

"Bast, we want Santa and his helpers to take gifts to all of the children, but we're scared. Why can't grown-ups help him? We're little. We want to go home. What would happen if we took our bracelets off now? Would we go home and would Christmas come tomorrow?" Claira asked.

"I don't know. Maybe you would just be back in bed sleeping? Maximus and I were told to help you on your journey and to protect you. We weren't told what would happen if you refused to go or took off the bracelets," Bast replied. "I don't know if there is anyone else that could help Santa."

Claira looked again down at the village. She looked up at the sky. No stars were shining, and she did not see the moon. The only lights were the distant twinkling of the lights in the village.

"Okay, we'll help Santa. I promised Mom I would always look after Ariel, and you don't know what would happen if we took the bracelets off. Besides, I have to take care of Kimberly, too. I'm the oldest!" Claira turned and stuck her tongue out at Kimberly.

Kimberly opened her mouth but closed it quickly.

Bast shook her head and held her right index finger to her mouth.

Claira stared at Bast's fingernail. It

was painted midnight black with a star in the middle. It had to be at least two inches long.

"Wow. Cool nails, Bast," said Claira as she nudged Kimberly.

Bast smiled and purred softly. "Thanks, I think they're pretty cool too. Now girls. We're all going to take care of each other. Maximus and I have worked together before, and we have never failed. We will take care of you and get you home before anyone knows you've been gone!"

Bast reached into the right-hand pocket of her beautiful coat and pulled out what looked like a whistle. She seemed to blow on it, but Claira could hear no sound.

"What...?" Claira asked.

"Why, I'm sending Maximus a signal, of course. How did you think we would get there? One toot means you've agreed to help; two means no," Bast said.

"Get there? Where? Aren't we *at* Santa's village?" Claira asked.

"No, no," Bast replied. "We're going to the caves, of course. If Santa were here, he wouldn't need us. He is being held in the caves."

Claira had heard no sound, but she

felt the presence of something behind her. She turned around.

It was Maximus. Claira smiled as Ariel turned around and ran to Maximus, hugging his leg.

Claira grabbed Kimberly's hand and walked up to Maximus. Claira gently rubbed him under the chin. "We're scared. I'm supposed to take care of Ariel. Kimberly, too. Can you take care of us?"

Maximus stood silently in front of the girls. His red eye was like a beacon in the dark night.

And then he smiled from ear to ear. *Smiled*.

"Bast and I will take care of you. You have already found out we have special abilities. Bast is able to change shape and travel through time. I, on the other hand, cannot change shape, but I have other skills. I am able to travel long distances quickly, without tiring. I am able to carry large loads on my back and to see great distances and through many veils with my bionic eye. Do not be afraid. You chose wisely."

"Hmph," Bast said. "Didn't trust me, did you? But a big dog with a silly grin wins you over! By the way, *I* don't chase snakes!"

Kimberly stared at Bast and turned to Claira. "I told you. She heard us! That's not fair!"

"I heard you, but I would not have interfered with your decision. I am not here to force you to do anything. I am a guide and helper," Bast said.

"But..." Claira stopped. Bast was smiling. Claira realized Bast was just joking around, not being nasty to Maximus. "My mom calls Labradors the 'laughing' dogs. I wish she could see Maximus smile!"

Claira turned back to Maximus. "Okay, we'll go. But you've promised to get us back before Nommy knows we're not in bed!"

Bast lifted each girl onto Maximus's back—Kimberly in front, Ariel in the middle, and Claira in the back. "You know what comes next, girls. Close your eyes."

"I want to watch," Kimberly said. "We know what you're going to do. Why can't we watch?"

"You can't. It's hard to do. I don't want to end up losing an ear or a tail!" Bast replied.

"But...I'm keeping my eyes open. You said you won't force me to close them!" Kimberly said.

"You're right," Bast said. "I can't force you. But on the other hand, I won't change until you do. We're going to get awfully cold if we just stand around here."

Claira, Kimberly, and Ariel closed their eyes. Kimberly snuggled close to Maximus's neck, Ariel inched closer to her, and Claira put her arms around Ariel and held her close. Claira felt Bast the cat jump up behind her. Claira felt the muscles in Maximus's back tense and then stretch as Maximus flew silently across the snow. He ran parallel to the twinkling lights of Santa's village.

Claira opened her eyes. The cold wind stung her face and made her eyes water. The only sound she heard was a soft purr from Bast. She snuggled close to Ariel and buried her head against her back.

Suddenly Claira felt a ripple going down the muscles of Maximus's back. Lifting and bending his front legs, he lightly sprang forward.

"Oh!" said Claira as she realized Maximus had jumped into darkness.

CHAPTER 8

THE TUNNEL

C LAIRA FELT MAXIMUS JUMP, AND she sat up straight and peered into the darkness. She could hear Ariel whimpering.

Claira squeezed her tightly around the waist and leaned to the right. She stared into the darkness. She looked down at Maximus and could not see the fur on his back. *Nothing.* She tried to pull off her glove so she could feel his fur, but her glove would not come off. She remembered what Bast had told them: the gloves had some special power that prevented them from falling off of Maximus.

Claira sensed they were moving very fast, but there was no wind. She realized she no longer felt cold snowflakes on her face. It was not hot, but it was definitely warmer than it had been before.

"Bast!" Claira whispered. The darkness was overwhelming. Claira was too afraid to yell.

"Shh, girls. Maximus knows what he is doing. Look straight ahead. Remember, I can see more in the dark than you," Bast said.

"There, I see it! A light!" Kimberly whispered. "It's like when we went into the closet with Bast."

Ariel had her face buried in Kimberly's jacket, but Kimberly shook her off, turning around slightly and giving a shrug. "Ariel, remember when we traveled with Bast into the closet? This is the same thing! We're in a tunnel."

Ariel turned around and looked past Claira. She turned back around towards the light in front of them. Ariel looked down at Maximus's fur. She looked at her gloves. "It's lighter! I can see my gloves."

Claira stared at the expanding circle. "Yeah, you're right! And it's brighter than when we went into the closet with Bast," she said.

"Close your eyes, girls," Bast said. "It will give your eyes a chance to adjust. It is very sunny where we are going."

Claira pretended to close her eyes, peeking out under her long lashes. She wanted to see where they were going. Kimberly turned around, and Claira saw Kimberly had squeezed her left eye shut but kept the right one partially open.

Claira felt Maximus extend his legs slightly, as if he were jumping over a barrel. She heard a soft whoosh and a click. Claira looked behind Maximus. The opening to the tunnel had snapped closed, and they were in bright sunlight over a stretch of beautiful blue water. The air was warm.

Bast was right. It was very sunny. Maximus flew across the water, low enough that Claira was able to see how clear the water was. She realized Maximus was gradually descending towards the water.

She spotted a pod of dolphins in the water. There must have been ten or fifteen, swimming and playing.

"Ariel, Kimberly, look! Down there!" Claira pointed to the water. "Open your eyes!"

Kimberly opened her other eye and looked down. "Claira...Bast...my gloves. They're gone!" she whispered.

Claira looked at Ariel and then at Kimberly. She looked at her own arms and then down at her stomach. Not only were the gloves gone, but her heavy coat was gone, too. She reached up and touched her head. *No hat.*

None of them had the winter clothes on, not even Bast, who didn't have her fur coat anymore. All four of them had on lightweight capri pants, Teva sandals, and light jackets. Bast's capris and Tevas were black, while the ones the three girls wore all matched. They wore pink capris with white jackets. Their Tevas were black with seashells across the Velcro. Bast had on the same kind of Tevas as the girls.

Claira reached over Ariel's shoulder and touched Kimberly's arm. "Cool! We look like triplets." She reached down and touched her own leg. "I like them."

"They're cool!" Kimberly said. She stuck her hands in the pockets of her jacket and found the clementines. She held one up. "Hey, they're still here! How'd that happen?" Kimberly asked.

"I bet Bast did it," said Claira.

"What? Nope. Was it in your pocket?" Bast asked Kimberly, frowning.

No, not frowning, Claira thought. *Just a funny look on her face.*

"Yeah. Ariel got them at Nommy's

house and I grabbed them before we went into the closet," Kimberly replied.

"No idea," said Bast. "Even *I* don't have all the answers. How many do you have?"

"Three. One for me, one for Claira, and one for Ariel," Kimberly said.

Ariel held up her hand and frowned. "But...our gloves held us onto Maximus. We'll fall off!"

Bast reached around Claira and touched Ariel on the shoulder. "You're safe, Ariel. Your capris have the same power."

Claira was so interested in their new clothes and the dolphins playing in the water below them she didn't notice the sandy beach just a few feet away until they felt a little bump. Maximus had landed gently on the sand.

Bast patted Maximus and slid her right leg over his back. She gracefully jumped to the sand. She reached up and touched Claira's left leg.

Claira jerked her leg away. She frowned and stared at Bast. "That's not fair, to scare Ariel."

Bast touched the other girls' left legs, and Claira and Kimberly slid off Maximus. Claira looked down at the sand. It didn't look like the beaches she was used to. She took a few steps. She knelt down and felt the sand. It was... pebbly. And sort of crunchy. Not the fine grains she was used to at the Outer Banks.

Bast reached up and put her hands around Ariel's waist. "Right leg over. I'll help you down. I'm sorry you were frightened. Claira is right. I should have told you what to expect."

Claira walked around to face Maximus. She rubbed him under the chin. "Thank you, Maximus. I wasn't scared...well, maybe for a few minutes. But we need to know what's going on before it happens. You know, for Ariel's sake."

Maximus smiled. "You are right, Claira. Bast and I did not think ahead. We'll try to remember."

Kimberly and Ariel walked over and stood beside Claira. Bast followed behind them.

Kimberly put her hands on her hips and frowned. "Will *someone* tell us where we are? First we go through a tunnel, have our clothes changed without asking us, meet some huge dog with a bionic eye, and end up in the snow near Santa's village. Next we go through another tunnel, change clothes again, it's summer, and we're standing on some beach."

Maximus smiled. "You are on the beach of Matala, in Greece. Do you know where Greece is?"

Claira stared at Maximus. "Greece? Yeah, I know where Greece is. We studied about the gods in school. It's far away. Nommy and Pa went there. They said it took all night to fly there."

"Greece? Gods? Where's Santa? I thought we were going to help Santa," Kimberly said.

"You are. Turn around. Do you see those caves? Those are the caves of Matala. Santa is in those caves," Bast said.

"Why is Santa in a cave?" Ariel asked.

"Duh, Ariel. Because he's a prisoner," Kimberly said. "Right, Bast?"

Claira frowned. "Stop being mean to Ariel, Kimberly. You're always making fun of her."

Kimberly frowned. Claira almost stuck her tongue out at Kimberly but decided she was the oldest and too grown up for that.

Bast shook her head. "Now, now, girls. Now is not the time to argue. We need to help Santa. And his top elf—he's here too."

Claira stared at the caves. There were lots of openings. "You expect us to go in there? No way," she said. "We'd never find Santa. And if we did, what could we do to help him? I don't like spiders and things like that. Spiders like caves. We hate spiders!"

"You're not going to be alone, girls. Maximus and I are here to help. Have we let you get hurt?" Bast asked.

Kimberly put her hand in the right-hand pocket of her jacket. She rubbed the clementines without thinking about what she was doing, then took one out and started tossing it up in the air.

Bast jumped forward and caught the clementine. "Kimberly, I'll take those, okay?" she asked quietly.

Bast turned to Maximus, smiled, and nodded once. Maximus nodded. Claira stared at Maximus. His bionic eye was glowing.

Bast held the clementines out to Ariel. "Put them in your pocket," she said. "Guard them carefully. They are very important. Even the smallest of us can play a big role." Bast turned around and winked at Maximus.

"Okay." Ariel put the clementines in her pocket.

Claira held Ariel's hand. She reached

for Kimberly's hand. What was going on? Why were clementines special?

Bast reached into her pocket and pulled out a ball of twine, but Claira noticed it didn't look like the ball Mom used to tie up tomato plants. Bast's twine was very thin and glowed. It glowed like *gold*.

Bast smiled. "We haven't much time. Kimberly, Claira, did your teachers tell you anything about the island of Crete and the legend of Minos when you studied about Greece?"

Claira looked at Kimberly. They shook their heads.

"They're young, Bast. It's probably taught when they're older," Maximus said.

Bast frowned. "Okay, it's like this, girls. I'll tell you about Minos and the bull later—"

"A bull?" Claira asked. "What—"

"Later! We have to hurry." Bast bent her head and loosened a strand of the shining thread. She used her sharp nails to break off a piece that was about ten inches long. She walked over to Maximus and looped the thread on the loop of collar under his neck. She pressed the ends together gently. They fused together. She placed the ball of twine in her pocket.

She turned to face the caves and began walking. Maximus walked beside her. Kimberly, Ariel, and Claira stood still in the sand.

"Are you coming or not? Santa is waiting," Bast called over her shoulder.

Claira grabbed Ariel and Kimberly's hands and pulled them. "You'd better not leave us, Bast!" she yelled.

CHAPTER 9

THE CAVES

B AST AND MAXIMUS WALKED SLOWLY, and the girls quickly caught up to them. They all stopped about ten feet from the cave entrance. Claira, Ariel, and Kimberly stood close to Maximus.

Bast looked up at the caves. They were yellowish and looked like they were made of sand. There were openings of different shapes and sizes.

She reached into her pocket and took out the ball of golden twine.

Claira stared at the ball and touched it. It felt as though it was metal, but it wasn't hard like the wire her dad had in his garage. It felt almost soft.

Bast took Claira's other hand and placed the ball of twine in it. "You're the oldest, even if only by four months. You will carry it."

"You always get to do the most important things, Claira. It's not fair!" Kimberly said.

Claira stared at Bast. Bast looked so serious, it frightened Claira.

She turned around to face Kimberly. "Here, you take it. I don't want it." Claira held out the ball of twine to Kimberly.

Bast shook her head. "Maximus and I were told you must be the leader into the caves."

"But..." Claira stammered.

Kimberly stared at Claira. She had never seen Claira afraid of anything. "Nah, I don't want it."

"You will do fine, Claira. You would not have been chosen if you were not capable," Bast said.

"Each of you has a role in our quest to help Santa, and this is Claira's. Kimberly has a different role to play."

Claira felt tears welling in her eyes. She quickly turned her head away and used her sleeve to wipe the tear running down her cheek. She couldn't let Ariel see she was afraid—she had to take care of her sister. She turned back to face Bast.

"Okay," whispered Claira. She closed her fist around the ball of twine.

Bast gracefully sat down and patted

the sand beside her. "Sit. All of you. We haven't much time, but I think you need to hear the story of King Minos. We are on his island, the island of Crete. It will help you to understand that what at times seems impossible is possible.

"Many thousands of years ago, people dug these caves, the Matala caves, out of the soft sandstone," Bast said. "King Minos was the King of Crete, and he lived in the Palace of Knossos. Matala is about ninety miles from Knossos. Minos was a good king, but he made a mistake and was punished by having a monster as a son. His son looked as if he were part bull and part man, and he was evil. Minos had Daedalus, a woodcrafter, create an elaborate systems of tunnels (a labyrinth) under his castle to prevent the beast from escaping. Supposedly no one could escape the labyrinth, and the beast could not be killed by arrows or swords.

"He was finally killed by Theseus, but then Theseus had to escape from the labyrinth himself. He was able to do so because his girlfriend had given him a ball of string, which he had unwound as he went into the caves. He used the string he had unraveled to find his way back to the entrance of the cave."

Kimberly stared at Bast. "I know what a labyrinth is! You mean we have to go into the caves, and they're like a labyrinth? We might not find out way out? Monsters?"

"Yes—I mean, no," Bast said. "The caves have many entrances and go very deep into the hills. You can get lost very easily, but you will have the golden twine. Claira will carry it and unravel it as we go into the caves. It will guide us home. And no, the monster who lived underneath Minos's Palace is not there. Theseus killed him."

"A monster?" Ariel whispered. She put her face against Claira's shoulder.

Claira jumped to her feet. "I'm not taking my little sister in a cave with monsters!" She hugged Ariel tightly.

Maximus approached Claira and stopped beside her. "Bast will be with you, Claira, and I will be outside guarding the entrance. As you have learned, we have special powers, more than you know. Minos's bull is not here, and we are here to help with any problems you may have."

"Promise?" Claira said.

"I promise," Maximus said. "We will

get you home safely, but only you three can help Santa."

Claira and Kimberly stared at Maximus. Kimberly walked over to Claira and took Ariel's hand. Claira gave Ariel another hug and reached for her other hand. She leaned over and whispered to Ariel, "Kimberly and I'll take care of you, Ariel. I promise. We need to help Santa. Bast is sort of weird, but Maximus is cool."

"Humph! I heard that!" Bast snapped. "Weird? I've been called a lot of things— like beautiful, stealthy, and graceful— but never weird!"

Claira kept forgetting Bast had such good hearing. She blushed but then realized Bast had a smile on her face. She looked at Maximus. He looked as if he was smiling, too.

Kimberly dropped Ariel's hand and stepped forward. She turned back and looked at Maximus and Bast. "I'm not afraid like Ariel. Well, not much anyway. I want to go home too, but we need to help Santa."

She started climbing up to the caves.

Bast watched Claira as Claira squeezed Ariel's hand. Claira turned and nodded once at Bast. Holding Ariel's hand, she tightly squeezed the ball of twine in the other hand. She turned and stepped forward, following in Kimberly's footsteps toward the entrance of the caves.

Bast looked at Maximus, flicked her long tail rapidly, stretched her neck, and jumped on his broad back. She daintily lifted her paw and pointed to the entrance of the cave. They quickly caught up to the girls.

Bast jumped to the ground and was once again a beautiful woman. She walked over to Claira. "It is a long, steep climb to the caves. Maximus will give us a ride to the entrance. He will remain outside to guard. Once inside, I will walk beside Claira, Ariel will be next, and Kimberly will follow Ariel."

Bast bent her knee and boosted the girls onto Maximus's broad back. "Close your eyes, girls."

"Sheesh, not again!" Claira whispered. Kimberly giggled.

Bast the cat jumped onto Maximus's back behind Kimberly, and Maximus began the climb to the entrance of the cave.

Claira looked down at the ground and saw only rocks and pebbles. The small stand of tamarisk trees was behind them. "Maximus doesn't even make noise walking over rocks," Claira whispered.

A few minutes later, Maximus came to a gentle stop. Bast jumped to the ground.

"We know, close our eyes!" Claira said as she squeezed her eyes shut.

"Okay, girls. Open your eyes. That wasn't too bad, was it? I'm getting better at this every time!" said Bast.

Bast was smiling as she helped the girls climb to the ground. She held what looked like a wand in one hand. She turned toward Claira. "Claira, take the end of the twine and touch it to the loop of twine hanging down from Maximus's collar."

"Tie it?" Claira asked.

"No. Touch it," Bast said.

Claira walked over to Maximus and touched the loop on his collar. It felt warm. She loosened a strand of the twine and touched it to the loop on the collar. The minute it touched the loop, it seemed to fuse to the loop, and the golden color seemed to be brighter. Surprised, Claira jerked her hand back.

Bast took Claira's hand. With her hand that held the wand, she beckoned for Ariel and Kimberly to follow. Gently pulling Claira, she stepped into the cave entrance.

Ariel and Kimberly hesitated briefly and then hurried to catch up with Claira and Bast.

CHAPTER 10

THE LONG WALK

IT WAS DARK IN THE caves. The only light was the soft glow of the golden twine and the wand in Bast's hand. Bast, with fingers on her lips to warn them to be quiet, stopped after they had walked about ten minutes. She turned around to look at the girls behind her. She held up the wand to point at some strange-looking drawings on the wall. "Later," she whispered. "We'll talk about them later."

They went into one tunnel, and it seemed to go on forever. They turned a corner and couldn't go any further. The passageway was blocked.

Bast held the wand up and examined the stone. "We'll have to go back, try another tunnel."

"Back? All the way to the entrance?" Ariel's voice quivered.

"Claira, rewind the twine and follow it back towards the entrance. You and Kimberly trade places so you are first," Bast said. "I will walk behind Kimberly until we return to the entrance. Ariel might feel more secure, to have the light behind her. The trip back to the entrance won't take as long since we didn't run into any obstacles on the way."

Ariel grabbed the hem of Claira's shirt, and they retraced their steps until they reached the strange-looking figures on the wall.

"Girls, stop for a minute," said Bast. She held the wand up to illuminate the images they had passed on the way into the cave.

"Drawings? In the dark? How..." Kimberly asked.

"Some of the paintings are very old," Bast whispered. "Maybe prehistoric cave dwellers or the early Romans. Remember, they had torches thousands of years ago. I'll tell you more about them later, when we're not in a hurry."

"I guess they didn't have a cat-woman who had gold twine and wands," Claira whispered.

Bast laughed softly. "Don't you think I deserve a thank you?"

"Nah. We wouldn't be in a dark cave if you hadn't come and gotten us from Nommy's house," Kimberly said.

Bast again walked in front with Claira as they explored each new tunnel. Ariel followed behind them and Kimberly was the last in line. While they were trying the third tunnel, Ariel tugged on Claira's shirt. "I'm tired. I want to go home."

Claira stopped, turned around, and hugged her sister. She kissed Ariel on the cheek and turned back around.

They turned a corner in the tunnel. Claira and Bast stopped suddenly.

Bast turned around to Ariel and Kimberly and held her finger to her lips. "Shh," she whispered. "Quiet, as a mouse! Tiptoes." Bast dropped her finger and turned back around.

"Wha...?" Kimberly answered.

"Voices," said Claira.

They stopped where they were. Even Ariel was quiet.

Bast turned around and held her finger to her mouth again. "Softly, girls."

They crept slowly to another turn in the tunnel. Bast stopped and held up her hand. "Stop," she whispered to Ariel and Kimberly. Bast peeked around the corner.

Bast turned around and took three steps back the way they had come. Bast stuck the wand in her pocket. She motioned for all three girls to come closer and leaned toward them to whisper, "We've found Santa and his chief elf! They're locked in a cage, playing chess."

"Chess?" Kimberly asked. "They're okay? How do you know they're locked in the cage?"

"There's a big padlock on the door of the cage." Bast peeked around the corner again. "And there are three trolls sitting at a table playing checkers. I guess they're the guards."

"Trolls? *Real* trolls? Here? Ugh, I thought trolls were just in stories," Kimberly said.

Bast looked at Kimberly. "Well, if Santa is real, why can't trolls be real?"

"I don't care if they're real. I just want to help Santa so we can go home," Claira said. "How are we going to save Santa, Bast?"

Bast put her finger on her cheek and looked off into the distance. "We need to distract the trolls, try to get the key for the cage. I saw a big key hanging on the wall behind the troll's table. Any ideas, girls?"

"Us? You expect three little girls to get some keys from trolls? You have magic. You do it!" Kimberly said.

"If we hadn't needed three little girls, you wouldn't be here," Bast whispered. "I can't do it, and Maximus can't do it. Think, girls. What can we do?"

Bast looked intently at the girls. Tears began to well in Ariel's eyes.

"I know!" Claira said. "We'll throw something and get their attention! Bast can change to a cat and jump on the table! Can you hiss, scratch them?"

"Can I hiss? Are you serious? Of course, and you will be very proud of me!" Bast said. "But...what will we throw to get their attention?"

Claira's face fell. Kimberly's face fell.

Ariel dug into her pocket and took out the clementines. "Here, Claira. Can we throw these at the trolls?"

She handed Claira the three clementines Kimberly had carried from Nommy's house.

Bast smiled at Ariel.

"Yes!" Kimberly whispered, pumping her fist in the air.

Bast smiled. "They will do just fine, little Ariel."

Bast huddled the girls in a circle and whispered, "This is what we will do: we will all go into the room at the same time. Claira will count. We will turn the corner at the count of one, enter the room at the count of two, and you three will throw the clementines at the count of three. In my beautiful cat form, I will jump on the table at the count of three and show them how scary an angry cat can be! Kimberly can run around and grab the keys. You three will run over to the cage where Santa is, and Kimberly will tell him to be ready to run."

"But...but...the trolls will come after us!" Ariel whispered. "They'll put us in the cage!"

Bast took the ball of golden twine from Claira. She unwrapped it further, then snapped off the end and looped it around Claira's wrist. The ends fused together. The golden twine that led back to Maximus was now attached to Claira's wrist.

Bast held the remaining ball of twine in her hand. "Trolls love gold, but not this gold. I will wrap them in the twine. They will not be able to get loose until two hours after we are out of the cave."

Claira shuffled her feet. She looked at

Kimberly and Ariel. She tugged on the twine attached to her wrist.

"Okay," she whispered. She turned and looked at Bast.

Bast told the girls to close their eyes.

CHAPTER 11

GOLD

ON BAST'S COUNT OF THREE, Claira, Ariel, and Kimberly ran around the corner into the room with the trolls. They threw the clementines, and Bast jumped onto the table where the trolls were playing checkers. Her tail stood straight up in the air, her fur was ruffled out, and she was hissing and spitting as she landed on the table. She held the ball of twine with one paw, and the end of it started to move through the air.

Kimberly ran behind the table and grabbed a huge key ring off the wall. Dangling from it was a big black key. Kimberly grabbed Ariel's hand, and they ran to the door of Santa's cage. Claira was right beside them.

But... as one clementine hit the table, another hit a chair, and the third one hit the floor, Bast heard three loud thuds. Bast looked at the girls, then at the clementines. Instead of three clementines, there were three shining balls.

Bast hesitated, staring at the balls, then turned back to the trolls. She continued to direct the twine to wrap them up. "Cat got your tongue?" she asked the trolls. The trolls' mouths were moving but no sound came out.

Ariel, Kimberly, and Claira looked at the trolls.

"Trolls have really nasty voices, and they say mean things," Bast explained. "As long as they are wrapped in the twine, they can't be heard."

The three girls turned back to the cage holding Santa and the elf.

Santa's head elf jumped up from his chair and ran to the cage door. Santa stood up, pushed his chair back from the table, and turned around. He stared at her and the gold twine snaking around the trolls. Bast couldn't remember if Santa had ever seen her in her cat shape.

"Girls! Santa! Take the key and unlock the cage!" Bast yelled.

Kimberly and Claira grabbed the key together, and they pushed as hard as they could. Bast heard a loud click, and the padlock came loose. Kimberly grabbed the hook above the lock and swung the door open.

Herbie the elf jumped out of the cage and gave the girls a big hug. He dropped to his knees and scrambled under the table to grab one ball, then ran to scoop up the second and third balls. Then he walked toward Bast. "It took you long enough!"

Santa stepped out of the cage. Claira, Ariel, and Kimberly stared at him. While their attention was elsewhere, with a soft *whoosh*, Bast was once again a beautiful woman. She stood in front of the trolls, holding the ball of twine.

Bast put her hand on her hip. She shook the ball of twine at the elf. "Ungrateful elf! Be careful or I'll wrap you up, too!"

"Humph!" said the elf. But he was smiling. He walked over to Santa and handed him the three gold balls.

"Thank you, Bast," Santa said, taking the balls in one hand. "And *thank you,* girls." He walked over to Ariel and kneeled down. "And *thank you* for being so brave and for carrying the clementines."

Santa stood up. "You have had a long journey and are anxious to get home. It will soon be Christmas Eve, and Herbie and I have much to do. But without your help I would not be able to deliver presents to the girls and boys this year."

He held up the three golden balls. "Do you know what trolls love the most?"

Ariel and Kimberly shook their heads.

"Gold?" said Claira.

"Yes, they love gold," Santa said, still holding up the three balls.

"But...those are clementines," Kimberly said. "Ariel snuck them from the bowl on Nommy's table so we could have a snack. I put them in my pocket and then Ariel carried them in her pocket."

Santa handed each girl one of the balls to hold.

They weren't clementines! They were heavy and shiny and they looked like... gold!

Herbie was dancing from one foot to the next. "Let's cut this short, we have a lot to do tonight!"

Bast frowned. "Who's the boss, you or Santa?"

Santa smiled. "Patience, Herbie. The girls deserve an explanation. We wouldn't be going anywhere without their help!"

"Yeah, what's this about...the gold balls?" Kimberly asked.

Santa turned back to the girls and held out his hands to the girls. Kimberly,

Ariel, and Claira placed the golden balls in his hands. He slipped them into the pocket of his red suit. "Do you know what a legend is?"

"How something started?" Claira offered.

"Close enough," Santa said. "Well, people are always wondering why and when we started delivering gifts to children, and..." Santa smiled. "There is more than one of us. The world is a big place, and one Santa and one sleigh would never be able to travel that far in one night! Even with Herbie's help."

Ariel frowned. "Are you *our* Santa?"

"Yes, little Ariel. I am *your* Santa. That is one of the reasons you three girls were chosen to help tonight."

Herbie frowned. "Move it along, or we'll never get back to the North Pole!"

"Forgive Herbie's rudeness, girls," Santa said. "We do need to hurry.

"One legend says Santa, many years ago, gave three golden balls to a poor farmer, so he would have money for his daughters to get married. That money to help them get pretty dresses for their weddings and to set up their new homes was called a dowry. I still give out three balls each year to someone who needs money to take care of their children."

"Bast told us about the golden balls and the trolls," Claira said. "They love gold! They wanted the three golden balls!"

"Smart girls," Herbie said.

"Yes, Claira, the trolls captured Herbie and me and were demanding the golden balls. But we didn't have them. Each year, they are given to us on December twenty-third, by the dwarves under the mountain. They are always delivered at eight a.m. sharp, but this year, they did not arrive. Herbie and I left at eleven to talk to the dwarves, and we were captured by the trolls."

"But...how... where were they?" Kimberly asked.

Santa turned and smiled at Bast. "Bast was on her way to visit Sammy, the dwarf who was to deliver the golden balls," he said. "She went with Sammy to the North Pole to tell me the balls had been stolen, and that is when she found out Herbie and I had been taken prisoner. She and Maximus are best friends, and she asked him to help when she got the note from the pigeons."

"But...how? Clementines? Golden Balls?" Kimberly said.

Bast smiled. "Sammy used magic. When the trolls took the balls they changed into clementines. The trolls were so angry, they threw them into the river," she said. "The Lady of the River took them to the little creek that runs through your Nommy and Pa's land, and the Wise Owl of the Woods delivered them to your house. Wise Owl is best friends with the pigeon who delivered my message," said Bast.

Claira stared at Bast. "You're the cat who was sitting on the windowsill at Nommy's when we were eating dinner! You ran away when I opened the door and called you. I was afraid you were cold. You were listening to us talk about going to the Walters!"

"Lady of the River? Wise Owl of the Woods?" Kimberly asked.

"Hurry! Bast will tell you later!" Herbie said.

"Claira, use your golden twine. Guide us out of the caves and back to Maximus," Bast said.

Bast pulled the twine tight on Claira wrist. She put Ariel's hand in Kimberly's. She grabbed Claira's hand and ran to the entrance of the room and peeked around the corner. Bast held up the wand. Ariel and Kimberly followed behind Claira and Santa followed them, Herbie bringing up the rear.

Claira and Bast led them out of the cave and to Maximus.

CHAPTER 12

HOME

C LAIRA WOKE UP AND RUBBED her eyes. It was dark out. She reached over Ariel and tugged at Kimberly's pajama top.

"Wake up, Kimberly," Claira whispered.

Kimberly pushed her away. "Leave me alone!"

Claira grabbed her again. "Ugh, Kimberly. I was dreaming...about Santa..." Claira looked at Ariel snuggled between them. Her left arm was flung across her chest. Claira stared at Ariel's wrist, then held up her left wrist to look at her own bracelet. She reached over and grabbed Kimberly's left hand and pulled at her bracelet.

She stared at the black cat on the

bracelet. But...there was another charm on each bracelet now: a golden ball.

Kimberly held up her arm and stared at the bracelet. She turned to Claira. "I was dreaming too...about Santa and this weird cat... And about three gold balls..."

All of a sudden, a breeze seemed to flow through the room, and Claira heard a low purr and then a meow. And then she heard a soft voice say, "Merry Christmas, girls."

Ariel's eyes flew open, and she threw the covers back. "It's Christmas Eve! Maximus got us home!"

Claira looked at Ariel and then at Kimberly. She looked around the room. No Bast, no tunnel, no trolls, no Maximus. She rubbed the gold charm on the bracelet. It felt warm. "Yeah, we're home, Ariel, and it's Christmas!"

Then she whispered, "Thanks, Maximus."

AFTERWORD

First and foremost I want to thank three special little girls – Kendal, Kyleigh, and Isabella. Watching them play and interact was the impetus for this, the first book in the series Museum Mysteries. I hope they never lose their delightful creativity and sense of wonder. They are like rays of sunshine.

Thanks to Glendon and his crew at Streetlight Graphics. Without their expert assistance the Museum Mysteries would not have been possible.

Thank you also to William Esmont, author of the *Reluctant Hero* series as well as the *Elements of the Undead* series. Although the characters in the Museum Mysteries series are not fighting zombies and chasing spies he has encouraged me to write what I enjoy – the adventures of three young girls.

Last but certainly not least I want to thank Misti Wolanski of Red Adept

Editing Services. Her advice and help has been invaluable, and I look forward to working with her on the next book in the series.